To parents and teachers

We hope you and the children will enjoy reading this story in English or French. The story is simple, but not *simplified,* so that both versions are quite natural. However, there is lots of repetition for practicing pronunciation, for helping develop memory skills, and for reinforcing comprehension.

At the back of the book there is a small picture dictionary with the key words and a basic pronunciation guide to the whole story.

Here are a few suggestions for using the book:

- Read the story aloud in English first, to get to know it. Treat it like any other picture book: look at the pictures, talk about the story, the characters, and so on.

- Then look at the picture dictionary and say the key words in French. Ask the children to say the words out loud, rather than reading them.

- Go back and read the story again, this time in English *and* French. Don't worry if your pronunciation isn't quite correct. Just have fun trying it out. Check the guide at the back of the book, if necessary, but you'll soon pick up how to say the French words.

- When you think you and the children are ready, try reading the story in French only. Ask the children to say it with you. Only ask them to read it if they seem eager to try. The spelling could be confusing and discourage them.

- Above all encourage the children, and give lots of praise. Little children are usually quite unselfconscious and this is excellent for building up confidence in a foreign language.

First edition for the United States, its Dependencies, Canada, and the Philippines published 2000 by Barron's Educational Series, Inc.
Text © Copyright 2000 by b small publishing, Surrey, England.

T 161873

Hurry up, Molly

Dépêche-toi, Molly

Lone Morton

Pictures by Gill Scriven
French by Christophe Dillinger

BARRON'S

"Come on Molly, into the bathroom.
Then I'll read you a story," says Dad.

"Allez Molly, dans la salle de bain.
Ensuite je te raconterai une histoire,"
dit papa.

"Carry me, carry me!"

Dad picks Molly up.

"Porte-moi, porte-moi!"

Papa prend Molly dans ses bras.

"Upside down?"

"La tête en bas?"

"Over my shoulder?"
"Sur mon épaule?"

"Or on my back?" asks Dad.
"Ou sur mon dos?" demande papa.

"Like a baby!" says Molly, laughing.

"Comme un bébé!" dit Molly en riant.

"Hurry up Molly," Dad says,
"I'll wait in your bedroom."

"Dépêche-toi, Molly," dit papa,
"Je vais t'attendre dans ta chambre."

"Wash your face," he calls,
"Lave-toi la figure," crie-t-il,

"and behind your ears."
"et derrière les oreilles."

"Brush your teeth."

"Lave-toi les dents."

Molly also brushes her hair…
Molly se brosse aussi les cheveux…

to the left…
à gauche…

…to the right,
…à droite,

…over her nose,
…sur son nez,

and all on top of her head!
et le tout au-dessus de la tête!

Molly looks in Dad's mirror.
Molly se regarde dans le miroir de papa.

Her chin is long,
Son menton est long,

...her eyes are big,
...ses yeux sont gros,

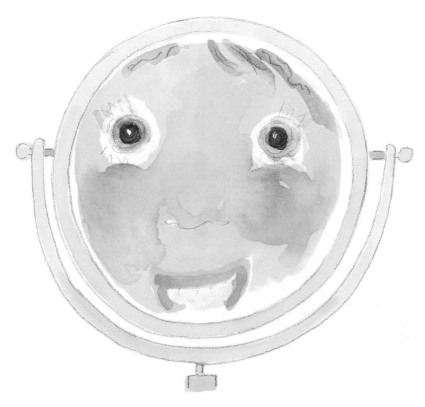

...her cheeks are fat.
...ses joues sont rondes.

What a sight!
Quel spectacle!

She puts some talcum powder on
her hand, and blows…

Elle se met de la poudre dans la main,
et elle souffle…

...and blows!
...et elle souffle!

What a mess!
Quel désastre!

She sprays some perfume
on her neck…

Elle se met du parfum dans le cou…

…and on her toes.
…et sur les doigts de pied.

What a smell!
Quelle odeur!

Molly suddenly remembers her Dad.
"Just coming Dad!" she calls.

Soudain, Molly se souvient de son
papa. "J'arrive papa!" crie-t-elle.

But guess what Molly finds
in her bedroom?

Mais devine ce que Molly trouve
dans sa chambre?

"Dad, wake up! I want a story!"
"Papa, réveille-toi! Je veux une histoire!"

But he's fast asleep and snoring!
Mais il dort profondément et il ronfle!

Pronouncing French

Don't worry if your pronunciation isn't quite correct.
The important thing is to be willing to try. The pronunciation guide here will help but it cannot be completely accurate:

- Read the guide as naturally as possible, as if it were English.

- Put stress on the letters in *italics*, e.g. pap-*ah*.

- Don't roll the r at the end of the word, for example in the French word **le** (the): ler.

If you can, ask a French-speaking person to help and move on as soon as possible to speaking the words without the guide.

Words Les Mots

leh moh

left
à gauche

ah gosh

right
à droite

ah drwaht

hair
les cheveux
leh sher-*ver*

face
la figure
lah feeg-*yoor*

eye/eyes
l'œil/les yeux
ler-yee/lez yer

cheek
la joue
lah shoo

ears
les oreilles
leh o*ray*

chin
le menton
ler mon*toh*

nose
le nez
ler neh

neck
le cou
ler coo

teeth
les dents
leh doh

head
la tête
lah tet

shoulder
l'épaule
leh-pol

back
le dos
ler doh

toes
les doigts
de pied

What a sight!
Quel spectacle!
kel spectakl'

What a mess!
Quel désastre!
kel deh-sastr'

What a smell!
Quelle odeur!
kel oh-*der*

baby
le bébé
ler beh-*beh*

talcum powder
la poudr
lah poodr'

perfume
le parfum
ler parfuh

story
l'histoire
leest*wah*

bedroom
la chambre
lah shombr'

bathroom
la salle de bain
lah sal der bah

A simple guide to pronouncing this French story

Dépêche-toi, Molly
dep-esh twah, moll*ee*

"Allez Molly, dans la salle de bain.
all*eh* moll*ee*, doh lah sal der bah

Ensuite je te raconterai une histoire," dit papa.
on*sweet* sher ter rakon-ter*eh* oon eest*wah*, dee pap-*ah*

"Porte-moi, porte-moi!"
port mwah, port mwah

Papa prend Molly dans ses bras.
pap-*ah* proh moll*ee* doh seh brah

"La tête en bas?"
lah tet oh bah

"Sur mon épaule?"
s-yoor moh eh-pol

"Ou sur mon dos?" demande papa.
oo s'yoor moh doh, d'*mond* pap-*ah*

"Comme un bébé!" dit Molly en riant.
kom ahn beh-*beh*, dee moll*ee* oh ree-*oh*

"Dépêche-toi, Molly," dit papa,
dep-esh twah, moll*ee*, dee pap-*ah*

"Je vais t'attendre dans ta chambre."
sher veh tat-*ondr'* doh tah shombr'

"Lave-toi la figure," crie-t-il,
lav twah lah feeg-*yoor*, cree*teel*

"et derrière les oreilles."
eh derry-*air* leh or*ay*

"Lave-toi les dents."
lav twah leh doh

Molly se brosse aussi les cheveux…
moll*ee* ser bross oh-*see* leh sher-*ver*

à gauche…
ah gosh

…à droite,
ah drwaht

…sur son nez,
s'yoor soh neh

et le tout au-dessus de la tête!
eh ler too oh-des-*yoo* der lah tet

Molly se regarde dans le miroir de papa.
moll*ee* ser rer-*gard* doh ler meer*wah* der pap-*ah*

Son menton est long,
soh mont*oh* eh long

…ses yeux sont gros,
sez yer soh groh

…ses joues sont rondes.
seh shoo soh rond

Quel spectacle!
kel spectakl'

Elle se met de la poudre dans la main
el ser meh der lah poodr' doh lah mah

et elle souffle…
eh el soofl'

…et elle souffle!
eh el soofl'

Quel désastre!
kel deh-sastr'

Elle se met du parfum dans le cou…
el ser meh dew parfuh doh ler coo

…et sur les doigts de pied.
eh s'yoor leh dwah der pee-*eh*

Quelle odeur!
kel oh-*der*

Soudain, Molly se souvient de son papa.
sood*ah* moll*ee* ser soovee*yah* der soh pap-*ah*

"J'arrive papa!" crie-t-elle.
shah-*reev* pap-*ah*, cree-*tel*

Mais devine ce que Molly trouve
meh der-*veen* ser ker moll*ee* troov

dans sa chambre?
doh sah shombr'

"Papa, réveille-toi! Je veux une histoire!"
pap-*ah*, reh-*vay* twah; sher verz oon eest*wah*

Mais il dort profondément et il ronfle!
meh eel dor profondah-*moh* eh eel ronfl'